For Lon and the baby ~ A. H.

For my brother, John ~ H. O.

First edition 2013

Library of Congress Catalog Card Number 2012954329
ISBN 978-0-7636-5314-9

13 14 15 16 17 18 TLF 10 9 8 7 6 5 4 3 2 1
Printed in Dongguan, Guangdong, China

This book was typeset in Aged.
The illustrations were done in pencil and watercolor.

Candlewick Press
99 Dover Street
Somerville, Massachusetts 02144

visit us at www.candlewick.com

When Charley Met Grampa

illustrated by

Amy Hest   Helen Oxenbury

CANDLEWICK PRESS

Dear Grampa,

We got a dog. His name is Charley.
He sleeps in my room. He's a fast runner
like me, and he's got the same last name
as me. Korn.

When are you coming to see Charley?
Bring a big suitcase and stay a long time
and I'll meet you at the station. My coat has
a hood. Look for a boy waving, that's me.

Love, Henry

Dear Henry,

I'll be there Sunday, and my train arrives at noon. My suitcase is big. Look for a grampa waving, that's me.

Now, about that dog. Is he friendly or fierce? I've never been friends with a dog before. I'll do my best, but no promises.

Love, Grampa

Sunday was snowy and Charley loves
a snowy day and he loves to go where
I go, so I called through the house,
"Come on, Charley boy!
Come on with me to the station!"

It's two long blocks and two short blocks
from my house to the station. "Wait till
you meet Grampa," I told Charley, and he
danced in the wind and his ears blew back
and I pulled my sled for Grampa's suitcase.
New snow was falling over old snow, and
Charley's tail was up in the air,
which is code for *I know
the way to the station.*

The station looks like a tiny red house,
and there's a bench outside for waiting.
Charley is crazy for trains, just like me,
and waiting for trains, just like me,
and I put my arm around Charley
and we started to wait.

We waited a long time. No whistle. No train.
No Grampa. Snow blew across the tracks, and
we waited some more . . . and some more . . .
and some more. Charley sighed. A lot. He
slid into a sad little slouch. So I talked about
Grampa to make him less sad while we waited.
Charley smiled when I said Grampa's the tallest
Korn with the longest feet and he snores wild.
He did not smile when I said
Grampa doesn't know how
to be friends with a dog.

WHOOOOO WHOOOOOOOO . . .
Far, far away the train whistle blew.
WHOOO WHOOOOO! Charley's ears
perked up and he sat straight up and I held
on tight—really, really tight—and all of me
shivered and Charley shivered, too.
WHOOOOOOO
WHOOOOOOOOO . . .
WHOOOOO
WHOOOOOOOO . . .

Grampa stepped onto the platform.

He waved and waved.

His cap was green.

"Here's Charley," I said. Grampa looked
at Charley, and Charley looked back.
A long time passed.

"Well," said Grampa,
"are you friendly or fierce?"
Charley barked once and smiled.
Grampa did not smile back.

Charley barked at the train for a while, and when it was gone, he held his head tall, which is code for *Follow me, gentlemen! I know the way home!*

The snow was deep to Charley's knees, and more snow came down. Faster! Whiter! Faster! Then Grampa's cap blew off! Spinning higher! Smaller! Higher! Smaller . . . smaller . . .

Charley chased the cap in the white
whirling snow. Chasing! Chasing!
And then he was gone.
CHARLEY WAS GONE!
"CHARLEY! CHARLEY!
CHARLEYYYYY!"
I was spinning in the wind,
and Grampa was, too, calling,
"CHARLEY! CHARLEY BOY,
COME BACK!"

And then he was there.
With Grampa's

green cap.

Grampa looked at Charley and Charley
looked back. A long time passed.
Grampa spoke first. "Here you are,"
he said, and then he said, "Nice to meet
you, my friend." The wind blew the snow
and Charley kept the cap.

That night Charley jumped on the bed
with Grampa. He looked in Grampa's
eyes and Grampa looked back,
which is code for

I love you,

I love you,

I love you.

They both fell asleep.

And Grampa snored wild.

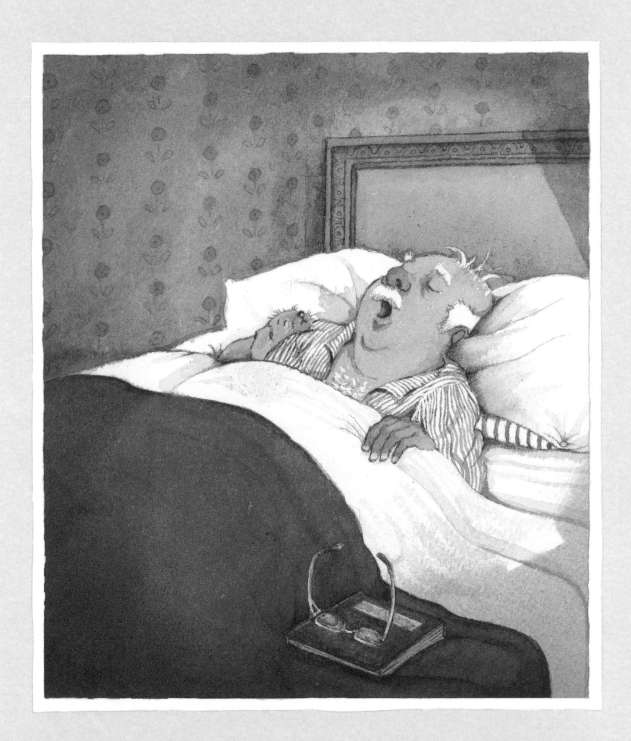